Peter's Place

Peter's Place

By Sally Grindley

Illustrated by

Michael Foreman

Andersen Press

*T*his was Peter's place.

All along the wind-torn beaches, all the way up the ravaged cliff face, this ruthless land's end was full of life.

Guillemots, shags, kittiwakes, eider ducks, long-tailed ducks, screeched and squawked and gossiped to each other, while in the turbulent sea below, seals and otters bobbed and weaved and played and feasted on the sea's riches.

Some came there to have their young. For others it was home.

They did not notice the distant procession of tankers. They were safe in their haven.

*B*ut it was Peter's place too. This was where he came to skim stones across the wave tops. This was where he came to search for crabs among rock pools. This was where he came to throw bread for the ducks and fish for the seals.

The eider ducks were Peter's favourites. They knew his call. They were not afraid of him. They knew this was his place too. He brought them food, and they waddled over to greet him, fighting to be first, though Peter made sure that none of them ever missed out.

But the time came when a passing tanker drew too close. Too close for the comfort of the playful seals; too close for the comfort of the cooing eiders; too close to miss the rocks that lay just below the treacherous tide.

Too close to Peter's place.

The scream of tons of metal smashing onto the rocks alerted the nearby farmers and jolted Peter from his sleep. They ran to the cliff edge and watched in horror as the stricken tanker broke its back.

*I*n fear for their lives, the men on board were winched away, leaving the tanker to fight its own battle. From deep inside its belly a foul-smelling blackness spread into the night.

When morning came, the blackness was everywhere. The waves frothed black, the once silver sands oozed black, the jagged rocks were covered in black slime that filled every crevice.

Peter scrambled down the cliff and stood where he had stood so often before.

A young seal, covered in oil, bobbed in the sea, its huge eyes begging for help.

*E*very new wave that crashed onto the shore spewed more and more bodies out, and left them all over Peter's place like mounds of unwanted rubbish.

A guillemot furiously plucked at its matted feathers, poisoning itself at every attempt to clean off the slime that prevented it from flying. An eider duck sat motionless and terribly weakened by its struggle to move.

Peter walked quietly over to it. He didn't want to frighten it. It was frightened enough. But the duck knew his call.

When Peter picked it up, the duck knew he wanted to help. It rested its head against Peter's chest while Peter cradled it in his arms, his silent tears carried away by the wind.

Then gentle hands took Peter's duck from him and carried it away to be cleaned and looked after. He heard his father urging him to join in with the rescue.

*F*or many days he helped with
the hosing and scrubbed away the
sticky slime that covered every
rock and filled every gully of his
childhood haunt.

Peter's place battled to survive.

*T*his is Peter's place now. Sometimes, when his duck comes waddling over to take bread from his hands, Peter marvels at its survival and smiles at its family sliding and tripping over the rocks.

And, sometimes, when he picks up a stone to hurl it across the tops of the waves, his hands are left sticky and black and the memories come rushing back.

*F*or, not far below the surface, in little nooks and crannies, between the rocks, under the sand, are ugly black scars that can never be washed away.

But, Peter's place is still Peter's place.

All along the wind-torn beaches, all the way up the ravaged cliff face, this ruthless land's end is full of life.